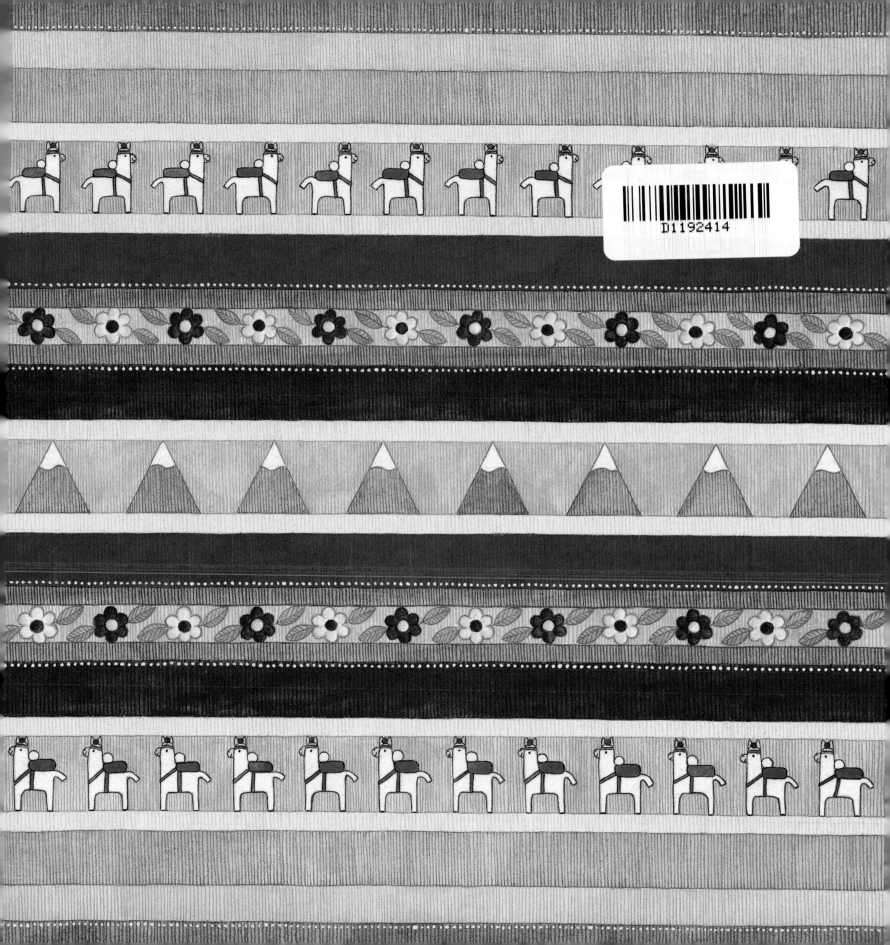

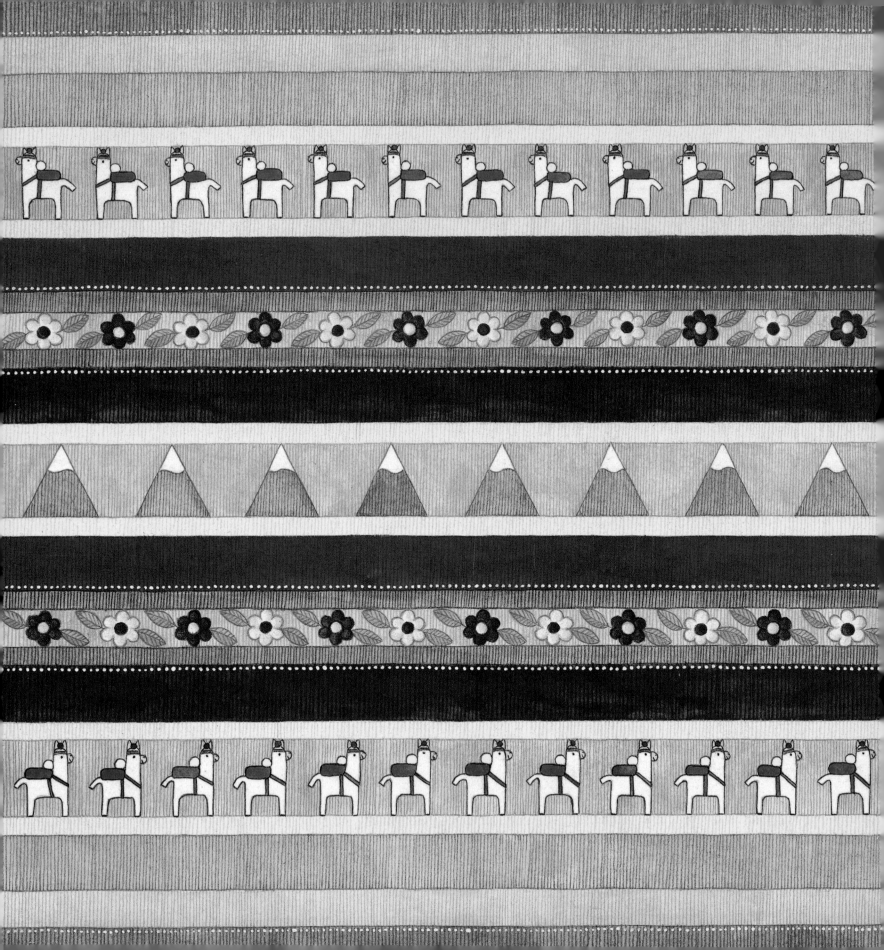

Macca
the
Backpacker

MATT COSGROVE

For all the dreamers and explorers — M.C.

Koala Books
An imprint of Scholastic Australia Pty Limited
PO Box 579 Gosford NSW 2250
ABN 11 000 614 577
www.scholastic.com.au

Part of the Scholastic Group
Sydney • Auckland • New York • Toronto • London • Mexico City
New Delhi • Hong Kong • Buenos Aires • Puerto Rico

Published by Scholastic Australia in 2021
Text copyright © 2021 Matt Cosgrove
Illustrations copyright © 2021 Matt Cosgrove

 A catalogue record for this
book is available from the
National Library of Australia

ISBN: 978-1-76097-846-4 (hardback)

Typeset in Mr Dodo featuring Festivo LC.

Printed in China by RR Donnelley.

Scholastic Australia's policy, in association with RR Donnelley,
is to use papers that are renewable and made efficiently from wood grown in
responsibly managed forests, so as to minimise its environmental footprint.

10 9 8 7 6 5 4 3 2 1   21 22 23 24 25 / 2

His favourite thing to do
is to **hang out**
with his crew.

There's **Al**,

Slow-Jo,

and **Dharma**,

the **Yaks**,

Rhonda,

and **Harmer**.

Macca also loves **drawing**

and dreams of ...
exploring!

So his friends helped him pack
everything on his back.

And one glorious day,
he set off on his way
on a **quest** to seek
the highest peak.

GOOD LUCK, MACCA
THE
BACKPACKER!

While, at first, our pioneer
was **grinning** from ear to ear . . .

soon enough
the going got
TOUGH!

When **Macca** wasn't sure
if he could go on anymore,
he imagined **Al,**
his **brave-hearted** pal.
And the path that seemed **hairy**
was no longer so scary!

When his spirits were low,
he gave **music** a go.
And the cool **Yaks'** soundtrack...

had his mood
bouncing back.

When it was too steep and muddy,
he could hear his gym-buddy,
Harmer the Llama,
cheer, **'You've got this!**
NO DRAMA!'

When he felt a bit weak
on the trek to the peak,
Rhonda's healthy snack
gave his **energy** back.

And lucky for **Macca**,
when his GPS tracker
sent him wildly **astray** . . .

Turn right . . .

Go left . . .

Circle back . . .

Dharma's book
showed the way.

NAVIGATING *by the* STARS

When he was aching and tired, **Slow-Jo's** motto inspired: 'To be **your best, you need your REST!**'

And a quick little nap gave **Mac** back his **ZAP!**

Macca's courage **shone**
as he soldiered on and on.
The alpaca didn't stop
until he reached the very . . .

... and took a **selfie**

(or **five**).

Macca

Al.Alpaca
Miss you mate!

H@RM3R
Champion!

Macca

Dharma_The_Llama
Brilliant Macca. So proud!

YAKS_N_SAX
Cool little buddy!

Macca

Slow_Jo_Sloth
Dreamy!

Rhonda_The_Anaconda
Are you eating enough?!

Then he captured the view.

But as Macca drew . . .

. . . it started to click
that he was **homesick.**

He was missing his crew.
But he knew what to do!

Macca pulled on his pack

and began the trek back!

He had scaled **HUGE** heights
and seen **great** sights.

But nothing could beat
the feeling so sweet
when he saw
his **friends'** faces ...

...and felt their warm
embraces.

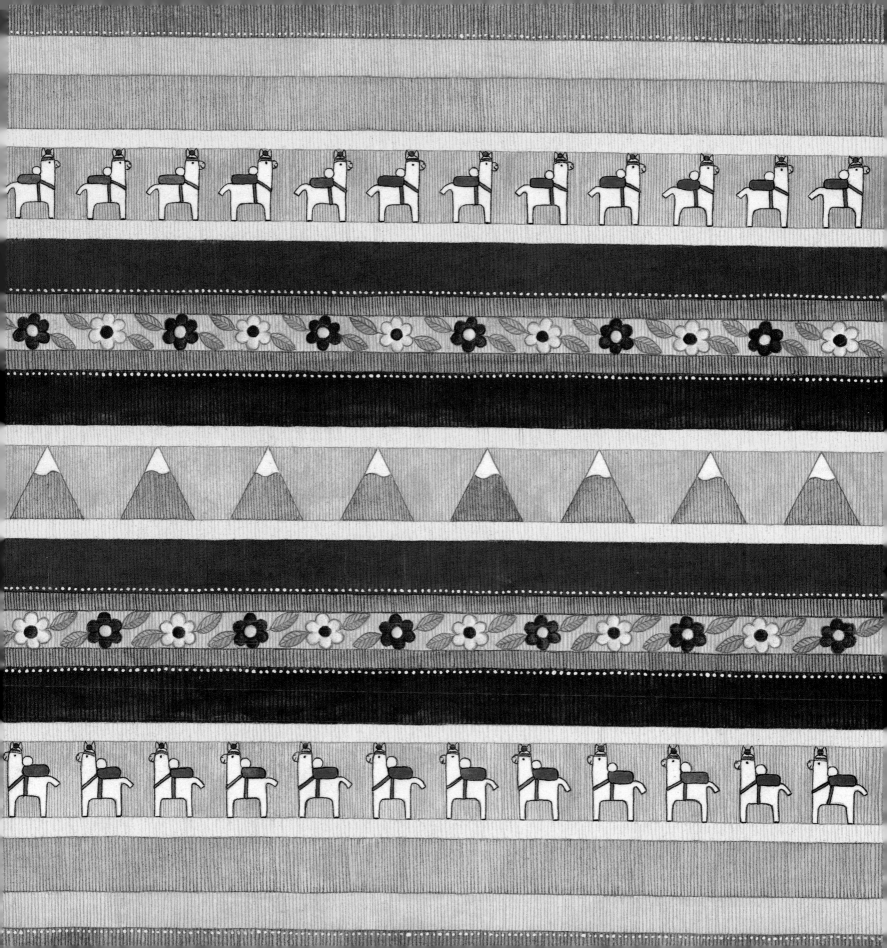

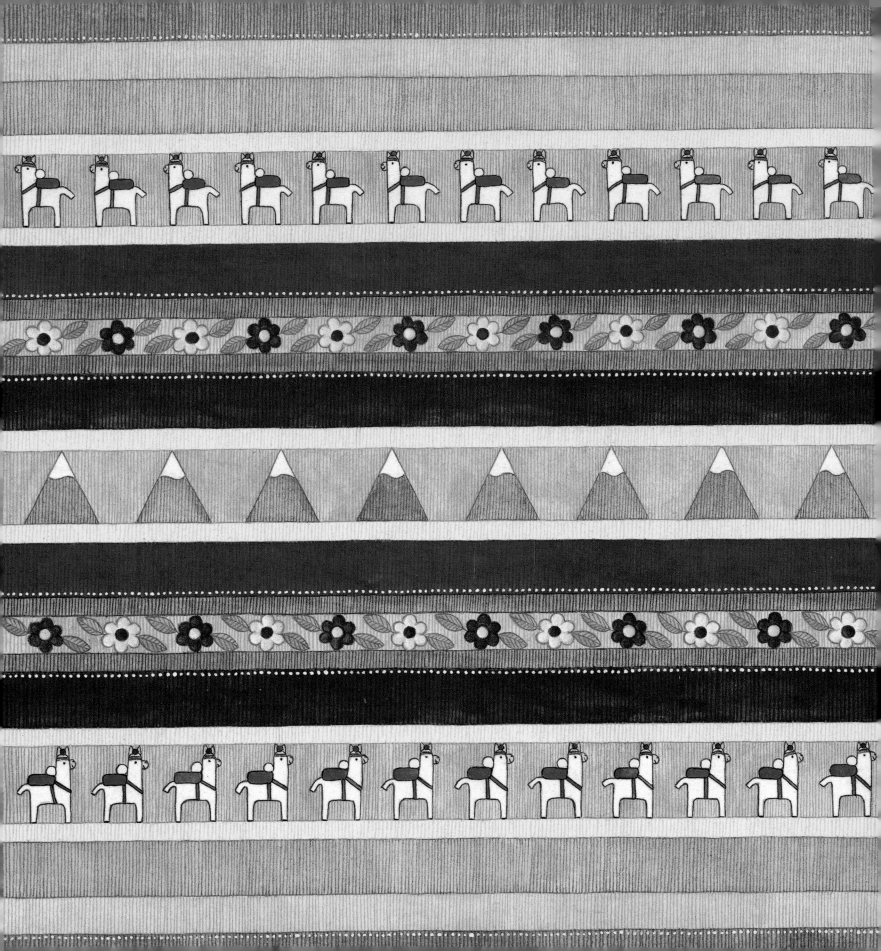